SCHOLASTIC
Phonics

The Fair

Published in the UK by Scholastic Education, 2022
Scholastic Distribution Centre, Bosworth Avenue, Tournament Fields, Warwick, CV34 6UQ
Scholastic Ireland, 89E Lagan Road, Dublin Industrial Estate, Glasnevin, Dublin, D11 HP5F

SCHOLASTIC and associated logos are trademarks and/or registered trademarks of Scholastic Inc.
www.scholastic.co.uk
© 2022 Scholastic Limited
1 2 3 4 5 6 7 8 9   2 3 4 5 6 7 8 9 0 1

Printed by Ashford Colour Press
The book is made of materials from well-managed, FSC-certified forests
and other controlled sources.

A CIP catalogue record for this book is available from the British Library.

ISBN 978-0702-30907-6

Author
Rachel Russ

Editorial team
Rachel Morgan, Vicki Yates, Abbie Rushton, Liz Evans

Design team
Dipa Mistry, Justin Hoffmann, Andrea Lewis, We Are Grace

Illustrations
Gareth Conway/The Bright Agency

Help your child to read!

This book practises words with more than one consonant next to each other, plus long vowel sounds (like '**br**ight' or '**agr**ee').
Read these words with your child:

street bumper complains Oscar Amber

Your child may need help to read these common tricky words:

I'm my we are going to the I all
I'll have of he says one love go so
some no

Before reading
- Look at the cover picture and read the title together. Read the back cover blurb to your child.
- Ask your child: *Have you ever been to the fair? What did you like most about it?*

During reading
- If your child gets stuck on a word, remind them to sound it out and then blend the sounds to read the word: s-p-ee-d, speed.
- If they are still stuck, show them how to read the word.
- Enjoy looking at the pictures together. Pause to talk about the story.

After reading
- Ask your child: *Do you think Dad loved the fair at the end of the story? Why?*
- *Which ride in the story would you go on?*

Can you spot the guinea pig on 6 pages?

I'm Oscar. This is my twin, Amber.
We are going to the fair down the street.

"I cannot wait for all the high-speed thrills!" boasts Dad.
"I'll have loads of sweets," he adds.

Bright lights greet us at the fair. "Let's start with the bumper cars," says Dad. He jumps in a green one.

We love the bumper cars.
Dad keeps getting bumped and jolted.

We go on the speed twisters next.

The man spins us. It is so much fun! Dad grips the bar tight. "I feel ill," he complains.

Then we all rush to the clown train.

It chugs up the steep tracks.

Then it swoops down and back up.
Dad frowns and looks a bit sick.

I spot the food stand.
"Can I get three scoops, Dad?" I say.
"Can I have some sweets?" Amber says.
Dad agrees.

"Have a sweet, Dad," Amber says.
Dad says, "No thanks."

"Let's go on that!" Amber exclaims, pointing at the helter skelter.

We go up the stairs. "The fair is fun!" I say.

Dad just groans.

Retell the story